W9-BSO-988

BAZAAR

BAZAAR

SUSAN WOOD

 HOLT, RINEHART AND WINSTON
NEW YORK

First published in 1981 by Holt, Rinehart and Winston,
383 Madison Avenue, New York, New York 10017.
Published simultaneously in Canada by
Holt, Rinehart and Winston of Canada, Limited.

Library of Congress Cataloging in Publication Data
Wood, Susan, 1946-
Bazaar.
I.   Title.
PS3573.O597B3   811'.54   80-14985
ISBN Hardcover: 0-03-057856-6
ISBN Paperback: 0-03-057709-8

First Edition
Designer: Amy Hill
Printed in the United States of America
10   9   8   7   6   5   4   3   2   1

I would like to thank the editors of the following
publications, in which some of the poems, some of them
in earlier versions, originally appeared:

Antaeus: "What We Really Are We Really Ought to Be,"
"The Names of the Dead," "The Disappearance"; New
England Review: "Learning to Live Without You"; The
New Yorker: "Bazaar: After Calvino"; Positively Prince Street:
"In a Field, In August," "That Light"; Sulphur River: "Red
Dust" (originally published as "Decade"); Missouri Review:
"After You," "As It Happens," "Elegy for my Sister,"
"I Want to Believe It"; Mss.: "The Failure of Language."

Special thanks to Yaddo, where some of these poems
were written.

FOR ROGER BROOKS
AND FOR CAITLIN AND CALEB

We ought to say a feeling of *and,* a feeling of *if,* a feeling of *but,* and a feeling of *by,* quite as readily as we say a feeling of blue. . . . Yet we do not; so inveterate has our habit become of recognizing the existence of the substantive parts alone, that language almost refuses to lend itself to any other uses. . . . It is, the reader will see, the reinstatement of the vague and inarticulate to its proper place in our mental life which I am so anxious to press on the attention.

— WILLIAM   JAMES

CONTENTS

BAZAAR: AFTER CALVINO

It is your one pleasure
in life, to go to the market.
To put on the veil of red
or lavender silk and walk out
into the light, to watch flies buzz
around mounds of raisins, to linger
for a moment beside plump bales of cotton
while cinnamon and dung steam on the afternoon.

But you go especially
for the night, when the women sit by fires
lit in the marketplace, their men
already asleep. Removing their veils,
they turn toward flames in which their faces
are reflected, and at each word a woman says—
lover, opium, bruise, mother, death—
the others tell, each one, their tales
of lovers, opium, bruises, mothers, death,

and you know that on the long journey
home, as you rock to sleep
above the camel's swaying, you will remember
the bright grief of mirrors, and as you gather
your memories around you like children
that were lost but are now
returned to you, your lover
will have become another lover, your bruises
other bruises, your death a different death,
so silently you don't even notice.

NECESSITY

You want to take your life
by its lapels, shaking it to make
it understand. Instead, you go on, inventing
as you go, the way words
invent the page, the way the dream invents
itself again and again, an overcoat

of heavy wool, yet transparent
as grief. It's the one you won't tell
in the morning, the one where the halls
are twisted in sleep, each opening
to another, where the thread you follow
leads nowhere. Those vague but tortured

disguises. You invent the idea
of what's missing as a room fingered
by winter sun where a man sits alone
by a window. He is dreaming of how
to change his life, and you
are the woman with everything

to lose moving toward him down
a corridor of snow: the endless
weather, night unraveling in your hands.

THE DISAPPEARANCE

In later years you will think of it
as sudden, remembering only how you turned
in yellow light and put
your arms around the air,
how you searched under the bed
and found a ribbon of dust.

The truth of my disappearance has slipped
through your fingers. Like the erosion
of stone by water, your body's sly
and constant friction, the way you held me
in the gravity of your obsessions. This
is what escaped you: the gradual vagueness
of my features, a shaft of light
through the bodice of my dress,
the loosening of my body
in the circle of your arms.

Now I am grateful, and think
of the slow abandonment
of love as necessary. To gather color
in the starkness of white, I wanted
one form as simple as light. As dust is.

THE SNOW DOME

Inside a paperweight, the world
is someone's idea
of a winter scene: white cottage,
white trees, white moon
like a single baby's tooth
floating in a blue mouth
of sky and over everything
a thin dust of snow.
This is where I live,
where I've learned to dream of nothing
outside myself. Here sounds climb through me
as a thief might
climb through an open window, softly
closing it behind him—the click, click
of a key turned in a lock,
the scratching of a pen
on paper, a cough. Hands
disappear, and the ache of red
tulips in a clay pot, until
what is left is only
the deliberate perfection
of sheets. The way frost
covers the panes,
bandaging the light.

Such limits
have their imperfections. Don't I know
how the silence of a body catches
in the throat? Still, I want the consolation
of pure loneliness, of glass walls

you can't break open.
I've come to dread the nights
you take the snow dome
from the shelf, turning it over and over
until snow rises into the sky to land
on a floor of stars, then rushes down
to earth again. I feel your hands fill
with longing, and you stare for hours,
waiting to see my face break
against the glass. Death sits in your palm.
Always it has been this way with us.

THE FAILURE OF LANGUAGE

It washes up in dreams, the way debris
is washed ashore, until I choke
on splinters of wood, taste sawdust
on my tongue, a sour death.
What I want is to speak
in tongues about your body,
to embody the untranslatable word
for love. But there's so much
I try to cover up,
sitting on my hands. I'm a child again,
choking on tears, while my mother stares off
at the horizon. Her eyes flicker.
It's not so bad, she says, it will be
all right. Or a child dies
in my arms. I hold her up and tears
pour from her mouth. I look
inside. The level of water
has risen to the roof.

AFTER YOU

1

Somewhere I wake in the dark.
The air doesn't move, waiting
for rain. Heat sits on my chest,
pins me down by the wrists, and I think
of endless, unforgiving summers,
the way we held anger
between us, like hands, like the death
of hands. Our bodies coming together
like fists, the bodies of strangers colliding
at intersections, the bruised and bitter streets.

2

There's another street, a window
glowing red at dusk, where you wait
for night to absorb
the last shreds of light, for blame
to strike against the pane
like a jagged, broken moon. I imagine
you sitting alone, bourbon and ice
in your glass, while any song
with the word *blue* in it
plays on the radio. Memory has its consolations,
the translation of an imagined event into the blue
the sky is some evening after rain, washed
with pink and gold like summer dresses.
Guilt plants its whiskey kiss on your lips.

3

Your father sits on the bed.
You can never do enough,
he says, touching your face.
In your hands loneliness shatters
like a mirror, and you want to walk through
mirrors, through walls, breaking everything
open. No one will ever love you enough.
Everyone has secrets. You listened in
on dreams, took them as your own,
your kisses breaking into my mouth,
stealing my breath.

4

Sometimes another man's lips move
like birds over my body, promising
everything. Or there's the promise
of despair, as when a woman stands
in an empty field one afternoon
in winter and her glance scatters
over the field like birds startled
by something both strange and commonplace:
the casual surprise of what we choose
to remember, a day shaped to any change
of weather, rain, our lives in danger.

5

I handle being alone
carefully, with attention, as one might
handle an unfamiliar knife, gently
running a finger along the blade,
measuring its strength, its weight
in the palm. The cutting edge is grief.
I have my secrets back, and breath
to stir the air with, somewhere
in the dark. It's a story where forgiveness
hardly matters, a story of knives
and rain: how memory cuts
into us, opening the soft place
at the heart of things.

THE NAMES OF THE DEAD

Thinking of them, you notice how light
leaks away at the edges of houses, how
the rim of dusk brims and spills
into shadows. Summer afternoons you'd say them over
and over, until the plump vowels, the angular consonants
took on the attitude of flesh: and *Della* and *Lois*,
your grandmothers, are girls again, dreaming
the faces of husbands in the blue opals of milk
that form in the pail, their sighs like sheets
drying in the wind. But it ends somewhere
in the lavender air of early evening, lamps
blinking on in kitchens and your mother's voice
calling down the lawn to the time
where you are always waiting, where the dead
rise, luminous, over the rooftops, leaving
behind them only the delicate bones
of silence in the slowly deepening night.

RED DUST

For Lois Lander Lee (1887–1931)

Perhaps you chose to remember
this day, to date from it as the day
things began to matter. Autumn's
incandescent air and the debris
of summer littering the yard:
the baby's red tricycle, a child's tea table
under the sycamore. In the only photograph
of you it is 1921 and you are falling
forward into the camera, into the first time

you will go to the sanitarium, the time
the family will move west to frame houses
floored with gray-green linoleum, to jobs
that don't pay, hired women,
and cures. In time, the world shrinks

to a screened porch, the bed a boat
you float in, your lungs clacking
and sputtering like oars pressed
into dark water. Pages from yellow tablets
billow in your lap, drift over the quilt,
and are lost. And always the tarps are raised
in summer, lowered in winter. Always

the high voices of children cracking
August's dry shell, and in the kitchen whispers
and sighs. Your daughters stir sheets boiling
in a black iron pot. The older one rubs

damp palms across her apron, and shyly,
like a stranger, she offers you tea
in a chipped enamel cup. Your husband brings

a plaid ribbon to tie back
your hair; his big hands smooth
the pillow. He does a slow dance
with his rented saxophone, and you
understand at last his need
to stretch beyond all he can imagine,
months of coins counted
in a glass jar. You try to think

of Saturday nights, the tub filled
for baths, emptied and refilled.
How water returns your body
to you for a while, how you soap
your pale belly, the thin black hair.
You want to forget the meaning
of solitude. Outside, the moon swells
with milk, and you dream of crowds, of armies
camped on winter hillsides. You dream
of a gun going off by accident.

When you move to the sanitarium
for the last time, you take only
the blue silk kimono your brother brought
from Japan, the delicate underthings,
and the fine lace handkerchiefs.
A week before your death you write:
At dawn I sit at my window and watch the sun
smear itself across the sky, red dust
on the mountains. I go back to sleep.

THOSE WOMEN, FOR INSTANCE

For Katherine Kadish

Those women, for instance, about to sail
the Atlantic again, in their blue
and brown woolen suits, foxes knotted
firmly around their necks, staring
so solemnly into the camera.
That stairway in the background
leads somewhere. As a child you thought
it led to one of those mysterious gardens
you'd seen in your grandmother's album.
Those patterned walks and perfectly
trimmed hedges, that English light
glinting off the still pond held there
like a china cup. Or the aunts gathered
on the lawn in their summer dresses, white
moths clustered at the edge
of the picture as though they would
fly away. Think of them boarding a train,
holding on to their cloches, sitting down
in the dining car, white linen
and roses on the table, crystal and silver.
Now they are about to re-enter
a past that closes before you
like the blurred and sodden pages
of a letter dropped in the garden
when a storm came, and you
are the tiny figure waving
from the doorway, calling *yes,*
yes, you were here.

THE END OF THE WAR

There has been a storm,
I think, but still
she is waiting for something
to happen, or someone.
It is autumn. Wet leaves
smear the stones, olives
fall like black pearls
from their necklace
of branches. She pulls
her thin wrapper closer
against the chill, and it
is autumn, 1945, my birth
nine months away.
In the distance the sounds
of ships, of whole fleets
returning. A man in dress whites
runs up the flagstone steps.
She turns as if to speak,
but the darkness overtakes
her, impervious as resignation,
though I will surely come
to know this fear
of arrivals and departures,
how everywhere, in the secret
and tiny hearts of stars, the past
is holding its own.

ELEGY FOR MY SISTER

1

Afterwards, it is morning and the pale bird
quivers in the bush, straining
to sing. The dandelion lists
on its stalk. I puff and the wind
hums with your name. I call you
Little Silence in the Grass, nothing
that ever was. The wind is the mewing
of a kitten drowned
in a sack. Morning, and my father
leans over me, his pitiful eyes
waxing with tears. He bends
to embrace me, and behind him,
in the shadows of our house,
the bush is flame,
the song, the feathers are burning.

2

See how I have kept it,
the morning of your birth
and death? I have hidden
it away among the baby things,
the delicate laces and the tiny gold locket,
while I thought of you
slipping into dresses I abandoned
on polished floors, your thin fingers
filling my rings. A tall blond woman
with many lovers, whose hands

make no mistakes. It is the breath
on the back of my neck, the echo
of a footstep behind me on the dull stairs.
It is the heavy stillness falling
from a sudden flash of wings, there, just barely
glimpsed, or the silence that shivers the air
after birdsong
on another morning of the world
going on without you, as it will
without anyone.

DESIRE

In the nursery the babies
are moaning in their cribs.
Little birds beat
beneath their skulls, wings flutter
behind their eyelids. They want to fly
away to another country.

Blanketed in their own darkness, the babies
circle the dim landscape, then dive
to the warm nest of the heart. They hug
themselves, their dreams whisper
another language.

Already they know something
is missing. Already they are folding
their arms around their lives,
holding on.

EDVARD MUNCH:
"OUTSIDE THE GATE"

For Caleb

The light must have shocked them, caught
them unawares, coming out of the stairwell.
It moves up the street, stretching away
from them into the interior, and the boy tugs
at the woman's hand, as if to pull her
with him there, fixing them
in that perspective. She must be walking
very slowly, the wind resolutely fluttering
the ribbons of her hat. Maybe her dress
is the blue of that odd thistle
splattering the fields above the harbor,
or it's the dull metal of the usual
Norwegian sky. What matters is the way
emptiness collects in the street, how it mourns
the future. Even then, she is dying,
though we may only imagine
that the woman bending toward the boy stiffens
with a slight detachment, already removing
herself, a thistle's self-defense
against an adamant wind. Soon the boy will begin
to cry, and go on crying. Outside, light
stuns us, too, who see the dark fragility
of children, of parents, who want to go on
living, as they did, for your sake, for mine.

SOAP

For Linda Pastan

The soap is the color of milk,
of bread fresh from the oven,
of lace curtains that hang
at the windows of the jeweler's shop
on Endestrasse.

Like the wax
of Chanukah candles
burning at dusk,

it is the color of snow,
the color of teeth,
the color of bone.

The soap rests
on the table beside the shower
where the officer washes
every night.

MODERN MEMORY

Give me the unchanging profundity
of nostalgia, love and death.
— JOHN CHEEVER

She thinks her best light is the light that dapples
lawns on late summer afternoons. The dresses are lawn
and the suits ice cream. The hats are boaters and she
leans out of the boat and lets her hand idly brush a lily,
curled and white against the dark water, while music
from the pavilion hovers over the lake and Chinese
lanterns blaze like fire opals in the trees. The moon is a
thin ribbon of indeterminate yearning. They sit on the
grass by the bandstand and suck on cherry ices. She
cannot imagine what husbands and wives do behind
the closed doors of bedrooms on hot summer nights.
But his arms are strong and he catches her when she
faints at the carnival freak show. When he kisses her in
the gazebo, she shivers and blushes. Sometimes they
drive to the lake in his father's new Pierce-Arrow, as
black and slick as a crow. It is 1913. In the fall he will
go to Yale or Princeton, she to Bryn Mawr or Welles-
ley. In the summer of another year, say 1927, she will
be waiting for her lover at teatime in the Palm Court.
She will be taking off her gloves, listening to the or-
chestra play "What'll I Do?" when she will suddenly
stop, hearing amid the music someone say the word
Verdun. It will be the first time she has thought of him
in years.

GEORGIA O'KEEFFE:
GHOST RANCH (1978)

Tonight the moon falls
into the mountains as an overripe
pear falls into an Indian woman's
dark shawl. As I wanted to fall
into his arms that day at Coney Island
when we'd just met. The sky and sea
and sand were one gray shape,
and cold. A lone red umbrella blew
down the beach. When he put his cape
around my shoulders, the villain
in every childhood dream (that black
cape, that black goatee!), I kept on
shivering. I wanted everything clean
and hard, loved the harsh sounds
of those German syllables, as though
if I called him *Alfred*, he would dissolve,
or I would. I would be a blonde

in a red dress dancing
on a table, my head wreathed
in smoke from expensive
cigars. I would sing
in a high soprano and men
would toss cut flowers
at my feet. The dress would be
red as these hills, my face
desolate and lovely. White

in the moonlight, the jimson weeds
have come back again, opening
their stubborn, delicate lips only
at night. Sometimes it frightens me
to think how deadly beautiful things
can be, and tonight I want
someone else's hand, another body
holding mine.

WHAT WE REALLY ARE
WE REALLY OUGHT TO BE

AFTER THE PAINTING BY
HELEN FRANKENTHALER

For Beverly Lowry

Imagine a woman
with a gift for centers:
how she moves to master
space by flooding it
with light that holds
the dark. That shape
says taking risk
is taking heart, that color
is a way of bending
time until it breaks
on a field of white where
what we are is what
we ought to be. The suicides
of her friends rise
on the air, and she dances—
she dances among them
like a woman who knows
what it means
to continue: to begin,
to begin again.

I WANT TO BELIEVE IT

I'd almost say there's no such thing
as history, that what we know
depends only on the hush
of spruce, this mauve half-light,
a stand of blue-black mountains defining a valley
where all the houses are yellow
with green shutters, ample rooms smelling of roses
and linseed oil. I told you once I wanted
closure, the formal patterns a Japanese garden
makes, the chaste shadows
of equal angles. But notice the smoked mirror
of the pond, how the light sinks
into it, hidden until the place where water hesitates,
then plunges, like a woman who's just stepped out
of her dress before a new lover, to a river
lost in trees. We found that river once, sliding
down a tangled bank, and agreed
it was worth it, if only because
that still, odd moment, those improbable chunks
of sunlight tumbling through the leaves,
seemed all the life
we ever wanted or believed in. But it always
fools you, that green humming
at the heart, time stretching away like a field
of blank, white pages. Even now, when our ghosts
are hovering everywhere, diving and swooping, self-
    protective
as the sparrows nesting in the eaves above our heads;
even now, when our pasts clutch us
like these moths grasping at the screen or words

that come and come and won't go away, I want
to believe it, want to whisper that history
is what we make it, fluid, never static, like water rising
to air, shared as this fractured light that bends
our bodies into such congruent shadows we can't
    remember
where we are. I want to believe it.

IN A FIELD, IN AUGUST

What I remember is in August,
the moon swollen
in a dark black and purple
as a bruise. We are walking
in a field, only our fingers
are touching. Behind us,
the mountains rise up, stiff
against the night sky, and the moonlight
is water filling the space we walk in.

You speak of your father
coming home each night tired
from the factory, of a childhood
you won't forgive. You speak of wanting
to give up your body, its cells,
to disappear into the bodies
of others. How it frightens you.

When I lean on your arm, it burns
through the cloth of your shirt, and I think
of telling you how I lived without a body
so long, a black dress full
of smoke. That now I know the body
is a form of grief, that fire
gives shape to suffering. But tomorrow

you will leave.
Now I want to lie down in the light
of that field, to lie down in my body,
to cover myself with your skin as with
the waters of a lake. To disappear against morning.

REMAINS

Though I cover you with layers
of leaves, with the high color of reality,
or the bodies of other men,
some things remain. Somewhere
you've just left and the screen door
bangs in the wind, stirring
birds that lift out
of trees, to whirl and dive
in the harsh silence. We go on
tracing bodies in the dark; our hands
linger everywhere. Still, I can't recall
your face, though I remember
any other. It has to do with need,
and longing, the way a child
in eagerness smashes the china head
of the doll she clutches, and it's no comfort
now to speak of time, its discreet pentimento,
an old painting in which this emptiness
may emerge as the distant figure
of a man striding toward me
down the broad avenues of the past.

LEARNING TO LIVE WITHOUT YOU

If desire is absence—the wind
whipping the bare branches, torturing
the sunlight so that it trembles
at four o'clock on a winter afternoon—
then absence brought us
together, and more than loneliness
divides us. The way our lives take on
the color of a Country & Western song, that blue
haze that smothers the interminable valley
like a scarf. Or a pillow on which
you dream each night of bodies
as rivers, your lungs filling
with flesh, of breasts parting

like water. I'd like to be the woman
whose lover wanted to reach
behind her ribs and cup her heart
in his two hands, but it's just you
trying to remember the origin
of your fear, what it meant to you.
You study your wife's palm lying open
on the quilt, the bones in your daughter's face.
You think of a trip to a museum, how I found
a postcard of Leonardo's *Last Supper*
hidden in Rauschenberg's *Odalisk*, or this
description of Matisse's cutouts: "As if
the hands that shaped those birds

were wings." Our letters cross:
words close over our heads like dark
pools. You take your wife's arm
and stand with her on the porch staring
into the hard shell of night, the snow
blowing across the road, rising up
the white body of the birch, into a sky
of blank and similar stars. None of it's true.
The night sky isn't a mirror absorbing
our light, only the space for stars
to die in. We both know there are two kinds
of betrayal. Even now, I dream
of choosing.

THAT LIGHT

1

In this green there is
a tenderness, Matisse said. White
wasn't tender, not
the brutal light he saw once
in America, gathering color to it
so that what seemed empty filled him.
The teeth of the world,
the color of memory.

2

My friend says women
write well about the past, but not
the present, or the future.
When we look at a man, we are seeing
someone else; when we listen,
we are hearing a voice behind us.

3

It was that light I saw
you in the last time. North
of the city snow still covered
the fields and light seemed to fly
out of them like startled
birds. The day stretched away
to the mountains. I remember

you wore a plaid wool shirt
with the sleeves rolled up. You stood
at the stove filling the brown plates. When
you had eaten, you angled your chair
away from me into the room, and began
to talk. What wasn't said

filled the space between us. A bird
stunned itself against the glass and you
lifted it out of the snow and placed it
on the porch. I should be happy,
you said; you were happy.
You spread your hands around
the room. I want to remember

everything: how, when I left, the rose-colored
ice was breaking up on the lake, spilling
in great chunks over the dam. Driving south
again, I saw green shoots by the road.

AS IT HAPPENS

Just as you're about to settle back
into the life you call your own,
it happens: the wind rubbing itself
against the skinny limbs of trees
in winter, the cold lips of flowers pressed hard
against the earth, and the lips of the dead
answering them, something sexual and bleak.

Too many small moments of comfort unfold
like useless handkerchiefs
in a larger landscape, an ocean perhaps.
This isn't the life you meant
to have, though sometimes it almost
makes you happy: a child nuzzling
your hand, your husband's soft breathing
beside you as the darkness
slowly backs away into a corner.

But in this weather you imagine
something else: there was a man you loved
once and you knew the consolation
of hard ground, the violence in the space
between two bodies that shocked you,
that turned your bones
to thin wires of light. And though

you'd thought differently, nothing
was resolved by the ice breaking open
on the lake, the vague shadow of green
under snow. A man's face is always
about to disappear and what's left
isn't enough. It never is.
Your own death is that faint
cloud of ashes on your breath.
You hold it, and go on.

THE REST OF THE STORY

For David Huddle

Even the air was excessive,
its envelope of heat.
She sat on the sand and stared
out at the lake. The deep,
motionless blue,
the abundant light groaning
with extravagance hurt her.
It seemed to have nothing
to do with her, only the false
promises of sailboats swarming
among islanded trees, the ordeals
of other lives.

She felt herself to be
the longing she was.

     *

It had something to do
with a story, or a landscape,
this life reduced
to sunning itself
under a white glaze,
a bleached
and self-contained sky.

Once it had seemed simple
to be without a landscape,
to come out of the flat

black land not knowing
the names of flowers
or trees, except the shadow
of the pink mimosa
staining the yard.

The others she had tried to make
hers by a ritual
of commitment, an approximation
of belonging. The purple hills
and pearl-gray rocks, little canyons
and arroyos wound by lost
caliche roads far to the west.
Later, the lights of the city
spread out like fire opals
on a counter, cherry blossoms
dusting the walks. East, mountains
shifting from green to blue,
forests of pine and silver-winged
spruce, the taut, white spine
of the birch. The necessary
particulars.

And what she didn't know
she imagined. South America,
its sexual odor. The exotic names:
jacaranda, bougainvillea, oleander.
Trains sliding down
the Andes, thick smoke raking
the sky, or the cut-glass solitude
of a single orchid in a bowl
in the Hotel Tequendama in Bogotá.

Beggars in the streets,
and the temperature threatening
100° on New Year's Day. Everything
turned inside out
like a beggar's hands.

It brought her back
to where she was. The lake,
the rampant light bearing down.
What she had lost
was the story,
what the landscape required.
In every one there had been
a man and woman.
They sat together at a table
spread with linen and their faces
promised something in the clean,
white arc of a lamp.
But who they were, or what
they wanted, she couldn't say.

      *

Everywhere the women
talked about men,
their fickleness
and charm, their boredom.

And everywhere the men
talked about women
and themselves,
their fickleness
and charm, and wept

with boredom
at their inability
to love.

*

She read these words:
"We tell ourselves
stories in order
to live,"
but could imagine
nothing beyond beginnings
because all the stories
were about love
and seemed to fade
at the points
of departure.

She remembered
her grandfather's story.
How, as a young minister,
he chaperoned
a Sunday school picnic.
The ideal silver boats
drifting on dark green water
swept by sunlight.
A sudden storm,
the lake puffing
and swirling, boats
dashed by a gust
like a giant fist.
Two lovers drowned.
She, a stiff, hand-stitched
shirtwaist, her straw hat

and parasol rocking
among the pink and white lilies.
He, his hair still neatly parted
in the middle, a white suit
bloated with water.
And how her grandfather,
telling his parishioners,
had said mournfully,
"And they found their bodies
two peet afart,"
and still blushed,
sixty years later,
recalling it.

And perhaps,
she thought, that
is the only story,
a disaster
reduced to silliness.
Perhaps the narrative
has been pulled
from under us,
like the Persian rug,
a gift
from the ambassador,
that her mother tacked
to the bedroom wall:
its exhausted blues,
its inconsolable reds
and spoiled greens
hanging there
beyond all possibility
of future use.

NOTES

"Bazaar: After Calvino"—This poem is an adaptation, not a translation, of one of the tales related by Marco Polo in Italo Calvino's *Invisible Cities*.

"Edvard Munch: 'Outside the Gate'"—Munch did a series of drawings with this title, all of them relating a walk which he took with his mother, shortly before her death, when he was five years old, and which he described in his journal.

"Georgia O'Keeffe: Ghost Ranch (1978)"—Ghost Ranch is O'Keeffe's home outside Abiqui, New Mexico. "Alfred" was her husband, the photographer Alfred Stieglitz, whom she always called "Stieglitz."

"What We Really Are We Really Ought to Be"—This is also the title of a painting by Helen Frankenthaler, owned by the André Emmerich Gallery in New York.

"The Rest of the Story"—"We tell ourselves stories in order to live" is the opening sentence of Joan Didion's essay "The White Album."